LAUGHING PAWS

BY NANCY BRYSKA

SHORT STORIES OF WHEN MY FURRY BABIES HAVE BROUGHT LAUGHTER INTO MY LIFE

DEDICATION

This book is dedicated to my darling Mum who inspired me to write this book, during our many conversations reliving memories or our beautiful animals past and present, she often said "We could write a book couldn't we?"

Well, Mum I have.

TABLE OF CONTENTS

INTRODUCTION

I have been lucky enough to share my life with many beautiful special cats and dogs. Each one has had their own special traits/personality. Each one has provided me with many special memories of times that they have melted my heart and brought tears of laughter to my face and to those of my family

They each hold a very special part of my heart and it is with pleasure that I share some of their quirky behaviours and unforgettable memories.

JAKE

1985–2000

Jake was a beautiful loving tabby cat we adopted from a veterinary clinic where my sister worked for many years. He shared our lives for nearly 15 years

NURSE JAKE

As a young girl, in school, during one of my physical education classes, I was involved in a game where we had to avoid being tagged by a fellow classmate, otherwise we would be sent to the centre of a circle for a period of time until we could re-join the rest of the group. On one occasion, I had been caught and had served my time in the centre of the circle, as I was about to re-join the rest of the class, I accidentally ran into a fellow class mate and we bumped heads quite hard. I needed a small butterfly band aid on my head and was sent home for the rest of the day.

As I was laying recovering in my bed, a young Jake decided to come in and offer his version of comfort and nursing. As he appeared on the bed, he noticed the band aid on my head and became very intrigued by it. He proceeded to jump and playfully paw at my head in his attempt to dislodge this peculiar item on his person's head.

Needless to say, this rough nursing care was not appreciated, and he was hastily removed from my room so I could recover in peace.

JAKE AND THE PENCIL CONTAINER

Jake, as many cats do, often found many interesting somewhat strange places to curl up and sleep for many hours.

As a young girl, I used to keep my supply of pencils in my room on a desk in an ice-cream container. On several occasions, after searching the house for him we would find Jake curled up in a tight ball in this small ice-cream container full of pencils.

We were surprised to understand how this could be comfortable for him or even how he could fit in such a small space without tipping them over.

THE HEATER HOG

As most cats do, Jake loved our heater. We had a space heater in the lounge room that was about a metre off the ground, about 50 cm wide and about a metre long. This became Jake's favourite spot.

To our human hands the top of this heater became very hot, but he would lay for hours on top of this heater, snoozing the winter woes away, only awakening occasionally to change sides and toast his other side.

On the occasions when he decided he had successfully warmed/toasted himself, he would relinquish this spot and come down to floor level to cool off a bit under the clothes airer nearby until he decided to return to his heater or venture outside.

CASSIE

MAURVILLE MADE FAMOUS

(KENNEL NAME)

1984 –1995

Cassie was my sister's sable and white collie, which we had the privilege of sharing our home with for nearly 12 years. She was a real lady and had a beautiful sensitive sweet soft nature.

NOT A FEARLESS PROTECTOR

There was one night where Cassie showed that in the face of danger, she probably was not the one to protect her people.

Cassie was in our back room chilling with my sister. All of a sudden, she came running in to the rest of us, who were in the lounge room, closely followed by my sister.

Apparently, something had fallen on the roof of the back room, like a branch etc. which made a large noise startling both Cassie and my sister from their activities.

Cassie heard this noise and with what would appear little thought for her owner, quickly ran from the source of the noise and ran to us for protection.

YUM! – KOOL FRUITS

Cassie, being my sister's dog, would often sleep in the bedroom with her. On this one night, my sister had gone to bed early to watch TV in her room and Cassie had joined her.

As a snack, my sister had taken a bowl of the coloured Kool Fruit lollies.

There was a brief absence from the room and the bowl was placed on the floor, on returning to the room, it was found that all the beautifully coloured Kool Fruits were now a slippery colourless white. Cassie had helped herself to the sweet delights and licked all the colour off them. They were too hard for her to actually eat, but great to suck and lick on!

TASTY PEANUT CRUNCH

During a visit to my local school fete, I bought a little peanut decorated with wool in Collingwood Football colours that was stuck to a little tile. I left it on display on a low shelf in our lounge room.

Predominately, Cassie would sleep with my sister, but she did have free range to sleep anywhere she wanted overnight.

The next morning when we awoke, we went into the lounge room and all that was left of my little peanut person was the empty tile, and remnants of coloured wool, no sign of the peanut.

Cassie had helped herself to a yummy peanut snack overnight

KELLY

CARAMANN BLACK SATIN

(KENNEL NAME)

1984–1996

Kellie was my mum and dad's tri-colour collie. She was a gentle fluffy giant who gave us all many beautiful memories over the special 12 years we had with her.

THE SMART EXERCISER

Kelly loved to play ball in the back yard, but she was very smart, and soon developed a clever way to play this game.

Whenever someone would throw the ball for her and Cassie, she would run together with Cassie to collect the ball, stop halfway, allow Cassie to run the whole way to collect the ball and wait for her to return halfway then "tackle" her, steal the ball and proudly return the ball for another throw.

She took pride in returning the ball to us, and was even prouder of the fact that she only had to run half the distance.

RUNNING HOME TO SAFETY

Growing up, I was lucky enough to have my grandparents live only a few streets away and we would often walk to their house for visits. There was a park between us and Grandma's house that we would walk through, and we would often take the dogs this way, so they became very familiar with this route.

There was one day, that Dad drove the short distance to Grandma's to help Grandad with something and he took Kelly with him. There was a vacant house for sale about 2 or 3 houses up from Grandma's.   On this day, Dad and Grandad decided to walk up to this house and have a peak at it, Kelly went with them and as she was quite well trained, she did not need to have a lead on for this outing.

While Dad and Grandad were poking around this house, they opened a garage door and on closing it, it made a very loud noise and Kelly was spooked, and she ran off from Dad.

Mum and I were at home and received a frantic call from Dad, "Is Kelly there??," he asked.

Not knowing what had happened we said "no, isn't she with you?," then we heard panting at the front door and were absolutely stunned to find Kelly sitting on the front steps, She had bolted from Dad and had proceeded to follow the path she knew through the park home to us. The amazing thing was that between our house and Grandma's there was a very busy road, so it was extremely lucky that Kelly managed to get across that road safely.

LITTLE MISS INDEPENDENCE

Kelly would love to sleep on her back on our couch or in the bean bag. It was so cute watching her sleep like this, but she was a solid girl and would sometimes find it difficult to get herself up, she would squirm around almost fighting with herself to get upright.

However, during these struggles, we were not allowed to try and help her by lifting her up, whenever we tried, she would get very cranky and grumble at us. We knew she would not bite us, but we could tell she was frustrated so we would just let her be and eventually she would disentangle herself and get out of her sleeping position.

Despite the struggles she had, she would not stop sleeping like this.

A COOL PLACE TO SLEEP

It was a warm summers day, and we had the puppy dogs inside to keep them cool, as usual they had free range of the house and could go anywhere they wanted to.

After Mum had attended to her daily chores, she thought she hadn't seen Kelly around for a while. She began to search Kelly's usual sleeping spots but couldn't find her. Even calling her name didn't end up with any response. Mum was getting a bit worried by now, she even looked outside thinking that maybe someone had let Kelly outside, but no, still couldn't find her.

She eventually went in to our bathroom, we had a shower with a raised tiled floor and a shower curtain. The shower curtain looked a little caught up, as mum reached out to straighten the shower curtain, she was surprised to find Kelly laying in the bottom of the shower having a lovely nap in the cool base of the shower. She managed to squeeze herself in to the shower base and was nice and cool. Mum was so relieved to have found her and decided to leave her be to continue her nap.

AN OVERWHELMED MUM

At the age of about 3 years old, we decided to allow Kelly to have a litter of pups. She was a fabulous Mum and gave birth to 11 beautiful puppies all sable and white in colour.

She was very protective of her babies and at one point we had to put newspaper on the glass door of the room where she was with her puppies because she got upset and over protective when our cat Jake looked in the door at her puppies.

On this one night, she was in the back room with her puppies during feeding time and we were all in another room of the house. Then Kelly appeared in the room with a pup in her mouth, she proceeded to place it on the floor in front of us, looked at us, turned away and returned to her other puppies.

It was almost like she was saying to us, "Oh my goodness, take this one will you, I have my paws full with the others and this one is being a pain in the backside"

So we picked up the puppy and helped her out by hand feeding it and then returned it to her.

NIGHT GOWN ATTACK

During the time we had all the puppies I also had pet rabbits in the backyard.

When the puppies were about 5 weeks old they were able to have their solid food for breakfast and spend some time outside. On this one morning, I was getting ready for school and I had to feed my rabbits outside, I was dressed in my PJ's and dressing gown and went up the back yard to the rabbit hutches. Well the 11 little puppies saw me and came running over to me and each grabbed on to the bottom of my PJ's and dressing gown, they formed a circle and I was stuck. I tried to remove them so I could keep walking, but as soon as I removed them they had all latched back on again.

I called out for Mum, and said "Help, I can't move", Laughing she came out to where I was stranded, surrounded by puppies, she removed my dressing gown, with the majority of puppies hanging on and once I was clear, she said "run!!". I ran back down the yard back inside and continued getting ready for school. Mum was able to successfully free the dressing gown unscathed from the puppies, feed the rabbits and all was safe.

JAMIE

DORINDALE COURT JESTER

(KENNEL NAME)

1987 – 1992

I loved all of Kelly's puppies but there was one little boy that stood out from all the others and stole my heart. Whenever perspective buyers for the puppies would come by, I would secretly hope that they would pick another puppy and not this gorgeous little boy. I told my Mum and Dad how much I loved this little boy and they would always notice me cuddling and playing with this little one, just a little more than the others. By the time the puppies were ready to find new homes, it was close to Christmas time, and Mum and Dad agreed to let me keep this special little boy who I named Jamie.

"I DON'T LIKE WALKING"

Jamie, throughout his life with us, was one of the very rare dogs that appeared to not like walks. We only could assume that maybe the fact that he was raised where he was born may have been a factor, as he never had to make the big trip away from his birthplace to a whole new environment.

Whenever, we bought out the leads or mentioned the word "Walkies" Jamie would run and hide, as if to say, no I don't want to go on a walk.

This is not to say that he never went out, he did, and he did enjoy his walk once he was out and about, but probably not as much as the usual dog.

"DID I DO THAT?"

Jamie, had such a beautiful goofy nature. For a number of years, we had 3 collies at home, and there were often some tense moments between the 3 of them often unintentionally caused between Kelly and Cassie by Jamie doing something silly.

Cassie, being a real little princess, was very sensitive about having her hair pulled. Now Jamie, being that big goofball he was, would walk by Cassie and unintentionally stand on her hair. This would cause Cassie to jump up and snap at Jamie. Kelly being the protective mother she was would not have any of that behaviour and would snap back at Cassie in retaliation. Then it was on, Kelly and Cassie would have a little "barney" although no real damage was ever done, we would have to step in and separate the two. All the while Jamie would stand by and look at them both, with a goofy puzzled look as if to think "What happened there?"

REDESIGNING THE BEDROOM FLOOR

Overnight, Jamie would sleep by my bed on the floor. I would close the door overnight to keep him in with me. My bedroom had linoleum on the floor. Jamie decided one night to take a liking to this lino and proceeded to chew it. He chewed it to the point that there was a big hole and he had ripped part of it behind the door which prevented it being open. So for a bit Jamie and I were trapped in the room, I managed to pull the pile away from the door enough to get it opened. Needless to say, Mum and Dad were not amused. The whole floor covering had to be replaced as it could not be saved. I ended up getting carpet in my room, which was lovely in the winter months. Luckily, Jamie did not find the carpet as appetising.

THE LOVE AFFAIR WITH JAKE

Right from an early age, Jake and Jamie had a special bond, they would often be seen laying near each other, there was certainly none of the traditional dog and cat rivalry in our house.

Jake would often lay and lick Jamie's face until it was wet. Jamie would come up to Jake, lay in front of him, gently nudge him and Jake would begin the grooming process.

Jamie was the only dog that allowed Jake to do this, there was one occasion where Jake walked up to Kelly who was laying on the floor having a gentle nap, he proceeded to start to groom Kelly in the same way that he would with Jamie. Although, Kelly had no problems with our cats, she did not appreciate this impromptu grooming session, and jumped up, gently snapped at Jake and he hastily retreated and never attempted to groom Kelly again.

On one occasion we can remember, when Jake and Jamie were outside in the backyard, Jamie walked up to Jake to say hello, and he accidentally stepped on Jake's tail. Jake was not amused and hissed at Jamie and tried unsuccessfully to run away. Jamie looked down puzzled at Jake and wondered why Jake was so upset, It was like he looked around and noticed he had stood on Jake's tail, so upset that he had upset his little mate, he quickly lifted his foot and Jake ran off in a huff.

Jake and Jamie shared this beautiful special bond for all of Jamie's short life with us. Unfortunately, Jamie developed epilepsy and at the age of around 4.5 passed away at home after suffering multiple seizures in a short span of time. After Jamie had passed, Jake come up to see his friend laying on the floor and give him a final sniff and was so startled to realise that Jamie had passed.

SAM

MANNAKAI SAMBOY

(KENNEL NAME)

1994 –2003

In 1994, my now husband and I moved in together in our first house and the time came to add a 4 legged companion to our home. Although I had grown up with rough collies, I had always had a soft spot in my heart for Labradors. As a young girl, I fell in love with a black Labrador that my Aunty had called Zara and knew that the new member of our family would be a Labrador. Our sweet little black boy Sam came to our home in April 1994, and soon become a cherished member of our family for close to 10 years.

THE LOOK OF APPROVAL

The night came when we were due to pick up our darling puppy Sam to begin his new life with us. Mum came with us for a short drive to bring this little baby home. He behaved very well in the car on the way home, only whimpering slightly. Once he arrived home, he began to explore his new home. It was dark outside so he could only view the inside of the house. He checked out every little nook and cranny of the house with a cheeky happy grin. He sat in his new little bed, and looked around his new surroundings, with what my mum would always say was an approving look, like he was saying to himself, "Yes, this place will do nicely, I like it".

THE DAY HIS NEW KENNEL CAME

The day arrived that our little Sam, was old enough to spend his days outside while we were at work. We placed an order for a special kennel that he could use.

It arrived one day when I was at work, my husband was home and was able to place it in position under our pergola. When I arrived home and opened the back door to have a look at the kennel, Sam rushed out, tail wagging and a huge smile on his little face. There was no need to encourage him to use it, he was so excited, jumping in and out of it and rushing to us as if to say "Hey, Mum and Dad, look what I've got, I love it".

From that moment on, he would spend many hours resting in and decorating his kennel with his own unique "chew art"

"ATTACK OF THE KENNEL"

Sam's kennel was designed with a split roof, that allowed the kennel to be opened and accessed for easy cleaning. There was one day that Sam's beloved kennel "attacked" and caused him a fright.

On a weekend day, I left Sam at home while I went to a family gathering. The weather was typical of a wintery day, the wind was blowing and was quite cold. On arriving home and driving in the drive and parking the car under the carport. I looked through the gates in to the rear yard and saw Sam running from the back of the house to greet me. As he became level with the pergola where his kennel was he gave a wide berth and stared in the direction of the kennel. I thought this behaviour was quite odd, wondering why he was looking at the kennel in this way.

When I got inside, and went to the backyard, I could see what had caused his almost scared behaviour. The back half of the roof was raised and stuck in the upright position.

I can only assume that poor Sam was resting in his kennel when a gust of wind pushed the roof of the kennel up and it would have been quite scary for him if he was inside it at the time. Luckily, this event did not upset him too much and he forgave his kennel and continued to use it. To avoid a similar thing happening in the future, we nailed the roof shut.

DEATH OF A GARDEN GNOME

Whenever Sam came to greet me, he had to have something in his mouth to hold or give to me, whether it be a toy, or even a piece of fluff or a leaf.

On one night, after returning home from work, I went out to greet Sam. He feverishly looked for something to grab hold of to give me. He spotted one of the garden gnomes I had positioned around the pergola. It was a small light gnome so was easy for him to pick up. He picked it up in his mouth and came running over to me. I saw it and thought, No, he shouldn't have that. I said to him "No, put that down", being the beautiful obedient boy he was, he let go and the gnome crashed to the ground. As it was not a solid gnome, it did not handle being dropped on to the concrete and shattered into many pieces. Luckily it was only a cheap gnome and it didn't matter that it was broken. I couldn't be mad at Sam, as he was only putting it down like I had told him, plus he had a beautiful little face that we could never stay mad at.

CHRISTMAS EXCITEMENT

One of Sam's favourite times of year was Christmas. He was just like a little kid when Christmas came around. It was something that was inherent in him, we never had to teach or coax him to enjoy this time of year.

When he saw us wrapping up presents he had the biggest smile on his face and would love to play with the empty rolls of the Christmas paper.

We soon learned that we had to protect the presents that were placed under the tree, as Sam would come rushing inside, go straight to the tree and rummage through the presents, select one and proceed to unwrap it, regardless of whether it was his or not.

On Christmas morning, we could give him his own stash of presents and he would eagerly unwrap them on his own.

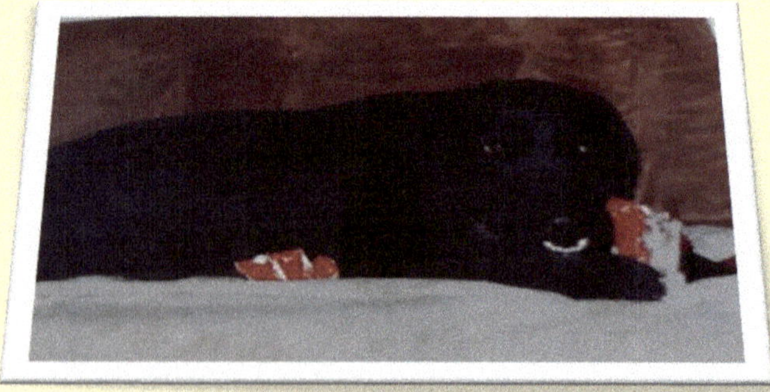

GEMMA

1997–2006

In 1998, it was decided, that the time was right to add another special member to our household. As I had always grown up with Collies, I decided the new member would be a blue merle collie. We found a beautiful special lady that was looking for a new home. She had recently had a litter of puppies and the breeder made the decision to rehome her after her puppies were fully weaned. We snapped her up and she became a special member of our house for many years.

At the time we rehomed her, she was already 18 months old, had no previous name, and had led a very sheltered life at the breeder's home.

We were able to show her a lot of new experiences and we could watch her blossom into such a happy beautiful girl.

HAPPY LITTLE GREETING

Right from day one, Gemma had a unique way of greeting us. She would gently snap her teeth together in a little smile. It was in no way an aggressive greeting. She would do this when she was really happy and excited. It was like her little way of giving a kiss. We would often look at her, see and hear her teeth come together in a little snap

LEARNING THE JOYS OF GOING FOR WALKS

Gemma, as she was to be known, during her first 18 months of life, had lived a very sheltered life at the breeders' home and had not had the chance to experience going for a walk on a lead before.

When she came to live with us, she was very timid and after a short settling in time, I wanted to take her on a walk in our local neighbourhood.

Sam, was a very confident dog, and I thought he would be able to help Gemma get accustomed to going for walks.

The first day we tried this was quite interesting. I put a lead on both of them and thinking Gemma would just follow Sam and I, started on our walk.

Well, this was all too much for Gemma and we couldn't even make it out the driveway. She sat firmly in the drive way and pulled to go back inside, while on the other hand I had Sam, pulling eagerly to start his walk. So here I was stuck in the drive way, arms outstretched to their capacity, one with Sam and the other with Gemma. Both dogs were determined to go their own way, and me stuck in the middle, having no slack to gain control of either one.

Eventually Gemma gave in and decided to come with us and eventually she learned to love walks nearly as much as Sam.

GEMMA'S 1ST DAY AT DOG SCHOOL

Due to the sheltered upbringing Gemma had experienced she lacked the socialisation that many dogs have the luxury of experiencing, and she was always a timid girl in social outings. To try and help her with this, I decided to take her to Dog Obedience school where she could experience more dogs and people.

On our first day, we joined a lot of new members and were awaiting to find out what class we were going to be in.   As we were all separated into our respective classes, we started to follow our new instructor and fellow classmates.   Gemma, was feeling overwhelmed and decided that this was not for her and laid firmly on the ground refusing to move. I tried unsuccessfully to encourage her up and to begin walking.   I could see my fellow classmates and instructor disappearing off to the training area.

In an attempt to keep up with them I lifted Gemma up and proceeded to carry her to the training area. Gemma, although, a small girl, was a fully grown collie and it was a funny sight to see a fully grown dog being carried to class. The instructor looked around and saw me carrying Gemma, he said to me "what are you doing? Put her down", I responded to him saying "She won't walk". He said, "put her down make her walk" So I did, and although nervous, she did agree to walk and ended up doing very well in her classes.

GEMMA HAS AN ADMIRER

At the beginning of each obedience class, we would all line up in a row and the instructor would come to greet each one of us and check that we had our collars and leads attached correctly etc. The instructor would usually have his own dog with him to help demonstrate the exercises we were all trying to learn. On this one day, the instructor placed his dog, a German Shepherd in a sit position in the front of the class and told him to stay while he performed his usual greetings. While the instructor was at the other end of the line to us, I saw his dog look over to Gemma and back to his owner several times. Once he believed the coast was clear he lept up and came running over to Gemma and proceeded to start playfully jumping at her in an attempt to get her to play.

Gemma and I were both a little taken aback by this, and as I was not completely familiar with this dog, I wasn't sure what to actually do.

I tried to pull Gemma away from this over friendly dog and then the instructor looked up and called his dog back and apologised profusely. All was well, and the class proceeded without any more problems.

It just goes to show that when cupid's arrow strikes and a dog falls in love with another, all the training in the world isn't going to stop a dog following its heart.

MACEY

2002 - 2021

It was early 2003 and we decided the time was right to add a feline to our family. Both my husband and I had always had cats in our childhood and we were ready to welcome a new member to our household. She was a very special girl, the first cat my husband and I have had the pleasure of owning together and was a very special part of our family for nearly 18 years.

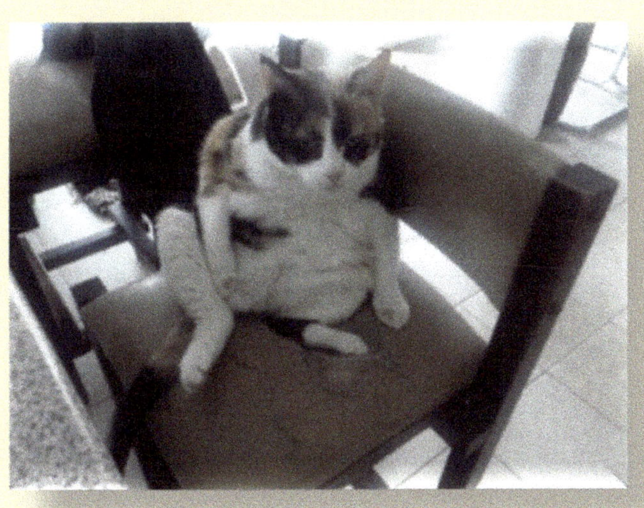

MACEY CHOOSES US AS HER PEOPLE

After the decision was made to welcome a little feline into our home, we made the trip to the local RSPCA shelter in Burwood. We were welcomed by the staff and taken to the cat enclosure where we could view the available cats and make what we thought would be "our decision"

There were many beautiful cats available ranging in ages, size and colours. My husband, who is very much a cat person, and is very quiet in nature kneeled down to look at the perspective cats and then this gorgeous little tortoiseshell girl came over to him and jumped straight up on his knee, rubbing against him. She then playfully jumped off, but her striking good looks and show of affection caught my husband's attention and he followed her and picked her up again to have another look. After looking at some other cats, I caught up with my husband on the other side of the enclosure and he told me what had occurred and said to me, I really think this is the one for us. After meeting her as well I was also mesmerised by her beautiful colouring and the decision was made, she was coming home with us and from that day on has been known as Macey.

MACEY HAS A FIESTY SIDE

Throughout her nearly 18 years, Macey had always had a feisty nature, which people have said is compatible with her tortoiseshell colouring.

As a kitten, she would like to hide under the bed and jump at our feet when we tried to get into bed.

She has always been determined and demanding for her food. On one night, I must not have given her the desired amount or type of food she wanted and when bed time came, she got quite annoyed and feisty and playfully chased me from the kitchen into the bedroom.

On one day she was required to have her teeth cleaned and due to the need for an anaesthetic, she was unable to have food for breakfast. Macey obviously not understanding why I was not feeding her, became very unimpressed by this outrage and became very vocal, following me around the house trying to persuade me to give her food.

She followed me into the bedroom while I was getting ready to take her to her appointment. She positioned herself between the bed and the wall leading into the ensuite. I attempted to walk past her and due to her being very angry and hungry as I walked past she jumped at me and bit me on the leg and then ran off, so as to show that she was very unimpressed by the lack of respect to her needing food.

I understood why she did what she did and all was forgiven, however when I left her at the vets, I did advise the staff that she was extremely cranky and that she came with a warning.

The only place Macey has felt happy and safe is her home, so on the occasions we went on holiday and needed to place her in a boarding cattery. It was very hard to find the perfect accommodation for her, in her younger years as she was always a little anti-social she would hide away in her enclosure and appear very angry to the carers.

Luckily for us, as she aged, she certainly mellowed and was nowhere near as feisty as she was and we have been able to find the perfect place for her to holiday when we are away, where she was very happy and content, so much so, that the carers can actually cuddle and even give her a kiss while she was with them.

THE DAY MACEY LOCKED ME OUT OF THE HOUSE

When Macey was a little over a year old she had a multi-level scratching post that we placed near our back sliding door that lead out to our pergola.

On this one morning I was getting ready for work and I had taken the dogs outside to go to the toilet before giving them their breakfast and leaving for work.

I closed the sliding door behind me, and while I was outside, Macey had jumped on the scratching post and leaned over on the sliding door lock, in an attempt to see where I was and when I was coming back inside.

In her attempt to gain a better look, she rested her paw on the sliding door lock, and somehow managed to manipulate the lock from the inside and actually locked the door on me.

I finished what I was doing outside, went to come back inside and found the door was locked. Macey was still on the top of her scratching post, looking at me, and meowing wondering why I wasn't coming back inside.

As I was the only one home at that time, I had no way to get back inside. My husband who was working a night shift was due home in about an hour or so.

We were living in a very new estate at the time and we had no direct neighbours. There was a new house being built next to us, so I was hoping that a tradie would turn up so I could ask to use their phone and call my husband to make sure he didn't take any detours on the way home so he could come home and let me in as soon as possible. However, on this day there were no tradies arriving at the property next door. My only option left was to walk up the road to the closest neighbour which was only a few houses up. The only problem was that the gates leading from the back yard to the front were all locked and of course could not be opened.

My only option was then to climb over the section of fencing separating the front and back yards which was a little over a metre and a half high and walk up the road to the neighbours.

It was probably about 7.00am by this stage and luckily I was dressed appropriately and not in my nightwear when I knocked on the neighbours door. You can imagine their surprise and amusement when I told them what had happened and they allowed me to use their phone to call my husband to arrange for him to come home as quickly as he could after leaving work to let me in so I could proceed to get ready for work. I was a little late but the reason was so funny that my bosses could see the funny side and all was fine.

Needless to say, from that moment on, the scratching post was quickly removed to another area away from the sliding door and I took care to ensure that the door could not be locked again if I was going outside.

MANY DIFFERENT SLEEPING SPOTS

Over the years, we have found Macey in many different sleeping spots around the house. She will usually pick one and sleep there for a few weeks or months and then go and find somewhere else to curl up.

We have found her several times in the bottom shelves of our pantry, even amongst our bag of potatoes.

We have even caught her once sitting in our dish drying rack on our sink.

We have found her in our linen cupboard, and even in our study cupboard.

She knows where she wants to go and will stand at the doors of these cupboards demanding us to open them for her. In her younger years, she would use her paws and open the doors herself by placing her paws under the door and pulling on them until they opened up

It is a joke in our house, when we ask where Macey is and the other responds, "She is in the cupboard".

As a young cat she would often lay on the back of our reclining chairs with her front legs hanging over the edge.

HOLLY

CLEMKIRK SUNSHINE LEAH

(KENNEL NAME)

2004 –2016

In 2004, shortly after the passing of our beloved Sam, we welcomed our 2nd Labrador, a yellow girl we called Holly. She was born early in January, so her name was inspired by Christmas Holly. Holly shared our lives for nearly 13 years. She was very agile and athletic, and had a very soft sensitive nature.

HOLLY THE HOUDINI

When Holly came into our lives, we lived on an acre block that had open wire mesh fencing. Being able to see the goings on in the estate was always so much of a temptation for Holly. No matter how hard we tried to make the fencing secure, Holly always seemed to find a way under or over the wire and would end up in the reserve that we backed on to. The funny thing was that even though she would get into the reserve, she couldn't seem to work out how to get back into our yard. There were many times that I would come home from work and find her sitting in the reserve up against the wire fencing waiting for me to come and get her back.

There was one day that a next-door neighbour found her in the reserve and caught her for me and I came home to find her tied to a garden seat we had on our front veranda.

VISITING THE NEIGHBOURS

During one of Holly's expeditions outside of our yard, she found herself in our next door neighbour's yard.

It was a weekend and we and our neighbours were home and our neighbour had her back laundry door open.

Holly, showing no manners, just freely went inside the neighbour's house. We heard a bit of excitement happening next door and then saw Holly coming out of her house, quickly followed by our neighbour. Holly was always super friendly and luckily our neighbour was fine with it, but she was a little shocked to see our dog in her house.

STOMACH OF STEEL

As would appear is the case with most Labradors, Holly could and did eat all sorts of things. She would eat her bedding, material and the most surprising to us was she ate dog collars

On a couple of occasions, we would come home and find Gemma or years later our next Labrador Ruby without their collars. We would look all around the back yard looking for them only to find the buckle left. The rest of the collar which was the leather type was gone, eaten. After losing 2 or 3, we gave up with having collars on our babies, and stopped using them.

We were always so lucky that these "tasty snacks" never caused her any harm and passed through without a hassle.

"NO, I WANT TO GO THIS WAY"

On our regular walks, when we reach a crossroad, I will often say to my doggies, "which way do you want to go, right or left?" so as to allow them to dictate the way the walk will go and add a bit of variety to the route.

On this one day, while walking Holly and our next Labrador Ruby, we reached a crossroad, and as usual I said to them both, which way do you want to go girls. Well Ruby, started to walk in one direction, so the decision was made. However, it appeared on this day, that Holly didn't want to go the way that Ruby had chosen. When I started walking in the direction Ruby wanted. Holly stood firm for a moment, looked at me, and this look came on her face like "I don't want to go that way". She let out a big sigh and then gave in and followed Ruby and I, taking one last look at the direction she wanted to go. I said to her next time we will go your way.

RUBY

BRADSHELL QUALITY LADY

(KENNEL NAME)

2006–2019

In September 2006, shortly after the passing of our dear Gemma, we welcomed a little chocolate lab puppy we called Ruby into our home. Although, experiencing the typical puppy shenanigans of chewing etc. Ruby was the easiest going Labrador we have had, she was always happy and never gave us a moment of problem. She grew up to be a solid girl, who we would affectionately call our big woolly brown bear.

GETTING LOCKED IN THE GARAGE

In our current house, our garage is separate to our house and located in the back yard. Whenever we need to come and go from our house we need to ensure our dogs are out of the way so we can manoeuvre our cars.

Both Holly and Ruby, were very well behaved girls and we could leave them in the yard while we moved our cars and there was never any risk of them escaping.

My husband who is a shift worker, often leaves for work mid-afternoon and on this one day, he had packed his car and was ready to leave to start his trip to work. As he backed out of the garage, he did not notice that Ruby had quietly slipped into the garage, he closed the automatic door as he always did, closed the gates and proceeded to go to work, unaware that Ruby was not in the back yard.

About 2-3 hours later, I came home from work, and noticed that only Holly was at the gate to greet me, which was unusual, as they were often both sitting at the gate eagerly anticipating my arrival. I called for Ruby and still no sign of her.

I began to worry, thinking that maybe she was sick and had collapsed somewhere in the back yard, or somehow had gotten out, leaving Holly the Houdini behind.

I hurried inside and went into the back yard, searching and calling for Ruby everywhere, still no sound or sight of her. I then had the thought, could she be in the garage. I opened the roller door, and out comes dear Ruby, tail wagging and relieved to be out.

As testament to her wonderful nature, there was no damage to anything in the garage that she had ample access too, no toilet mess, we are assuming that as it would have been very dark in there with the door closed, she would have just laid down and had a snooze, knowing and trusting that someone would soon be home to let her out again.

ASKING FOR TREATS

As all Labradors, Ruby loved her treats and snacks. She knew where they were placed in the pantry and if the door was left slightly open, she would nudge it all the way open, enter the pantry and search the treat shelf and make her selection.

Once a treat was selected, she was always so polite and respectful, instead of taking the treats away and busily eating them, she would carry them in her mouth, come and find one of us and show us what she had and wait for us to say "Yes you can have that".

There was one night, I was in the study, on the phone, and I saw Ruby come in looking for me, I was deep in conversation, so I didn't respond to her. She turned away and left, only to return a little while later. Again, I failed to respond to her. This went on for another couple of times. In the end, she gave up coming into me.

When I had finally finished my phone call and came out into the kitchen, I noticed the remnants of a treat box, with the treats gone.

All I could do was laugh, as I had been aware that Ruby had come in to ask me several times, in the end she thought, "Oh well, I did ask, you didn't respond, so I am going to eat these anyway." I just hope that she ended up sharing her stash with Holly!

THE YEAR SHE MISSED CHRISTMAS

It was Christmas eve, 2018 and Ruby was nearly 12.5 years old and wasn't as active and alert as she was when she was younger.

It was a warm day and she always felt the heat.

My mum was visiting and after dinner we let the dogs inside with us and shortly we were going to open our presents for Christmas.

Ruby was tired, and laid on the cool tiles for a little nap. She fell asleep and the time came to open the presents. We let her sleep and proceeded with the gift giving and unwrapping. As we were admiring our gifts, Ruby woke up and came in to see us in the lounge room.

Although she was never as fully excited by Christmas as our first Labrador Sam, she did enjoy the presents and pulling off the wrapping paper.

We could tell by her body language and face when she entered the lounge room that she was sad when she discovered that she had missed the present unwrapping. Her head hung low as she moved around the room sniffing at the empty paper and checking each person's stash.

It really was like she was so sad she had missed the Christmas unwrapping. We had saved her presents for her so she didn't miss out completely

FLETCHER

2008 – 2022

Early in 2009, I decided that the time was right to add another cat to our household, we knew we had room in our hearts and home for another little soul. I went to the local animal shelter to choose our new family member. Fletcher, a darling little tabby and white kitten became our newest family member.

HOW FLETCHER WAS CHOSEN

When I decided to introduce a new cat to the household, I had to be mindful of Macey's feisty personality. I was worried that she would intimidate and frighten a new comer into her territory. I made the trip to the local animal shelter and began to view the perspective cats. I noticed this beautiful little tabby and white boy. He was together with other cats in an enclosure. The other cats were attempting to eat out of a bowl, and this little tabby kitten came over and used his paw to push the other cats out of the bowl so he could reach the bowl and eat himself.

Seeing this, I thought, this little guy can stand up for himself, Macey shouldn't be able to intimidate him. So, this little guy was the chosen one and came home that day with us.

As all our other animals at the time had names ending in "Y" (Holly, Macey, Ruby), we decided we wanted something different for this little boy. So, we thought of other names and Fletcher was the one that we both agreed on

HUSBAND NEEDED ONLY A LITTLE CONVINCING

When I decided to add Fletcher to our home, my husband was not completely convinced, although he loved cats dearly, he was worried about upsetting Macey, and the overall harmony of the house, by adding a new cat to the mix.

When I went to choose Fletcher, the instruction from my husband was, that it would be on a month's trial, if Macey did not approve of this new addition, then he would have to be returned.

When I arrived home with this little young bundle of fluff, my husband was almost instantly hooked.

At the time Fletcher came home he had a mild case of cat flu, and was a bit snuffly and sneezy, which added to his cuteness, and made us fall in love with him that little bit more as he was a little unwell and needed us to care for him

Macey was not overly impressed and kept her distance, but when they were close by, Fletcher was easily able to stand his ground and was not intimidated by Macey at all, which is what we were hoping for.

As my husband is really a big softy, he quickly fell in love with Fletcher and after only being home with us for 24 hours, my husband said, "Too bad if Macey doesn't really like Fletcher, this guy is not going anywhere" So the decision was final, Fletcher was here to stay and from that point, Fletcher and my husband shared a special bond and were very close.

THE FRIENDLY HOST

As a young cat, Fletcher was quite social with the neighbour's cats, there were never any cat fights. He was so friendly that he had no problem inviting his feline friends home and inside our house.

Fletcher was mostly trained to stay in our own back yard when we were home, but there were occasions when he would escape from our house and venture into neighbouring yards.

He had made friends with our next door neighbours ginger cat and would often invite this friend home, and when we were home we often left the back door slightly ajar so he could come and go as he pleased.

There was one day that while socialising with the neighbouring cat, Fletcher came inside and his new friend followed him. Macey, not as friendly and social as Fletcher took offence to this unwanted guest and quickly chased him out of the house and back into his own yard, but in her desire to be rid of this guest, inadvertently found herself over the fence and at a loss in a strange back yard. She was shocked to find herself here and we had to go next door and rescue her and bring her back to her own home

"WHO'S KNEE AM I SITTING ON??"

Out of our 2 cats, Fletcher has always been the more affectionate and will happily curl up on a lap for hours snoozing the time away.

On one night when my parents were visiting, Dad was sitting in what usually was my husband's chair. Fletcher saw that there was now a knee available to curl up on, jumped up and began to settle down for a rest.

A little while later, my husband got up and was standing in the door way talking to us. Fletcher looked up at him and then all of a sudden a surprised look appeared over his face, he stared widely at my husband. He really thought that he was sitting on my husband's knee, Although he didn't move, we could see him staring at my husband as if too think, "what are you doing over there? If you are over there, then who the heck am I sitting on??"

Despite his concern, he stayed where he was, he obviously could sense that my Dad was also an animal lover and decided, Ok, I will stay where I am.

THE PLASTIC BAG ATTACK

Both cats love their food, and will think nothing of helping themselves to table scraps, even to the point of literally taking food direct from your plate if they want to.

One evening as my husband and I sat down to our dinner of Chicken meatloaf and vegetables, there was a loud commotion coming from the kitchen.

While preparing dinner, I placed the vegetable peelings and scraps into a plastic bag and left it on the kitchen bench to later be thrown out. We had also scraped a little of the left over meatloaf from the cooking tray into this bag.

While we were eating, Fletcher had jumped up on the bench and began to examine the contents of this bag. Unfortunately, he became stuck in the handles of the bag. This gave him a fright and he jumped off the bench and began running through the house with this bag attached to him, all the while the food scraps were falling out everywhere on the floor behind him.

Seeing and hearing his dilemma, we quickly tried to catch him to be able to disentangle him from the bag. At the immediate time, it was worrying as the poor little boy was quite panicked. After catching him and freeing him from his scary predator, my husband and I were able to see the funny side of it especially as we saw all the scraps emptied from the bag all over our floor.

Needless to say, from that point on, we have been very careful leaving scrap bags within his reach.

RAFFIE

LABZTALES MR SMARTY PANTS
(KENNEL NAME)

(ALSO KNOWN AS MR VANDAL PANTS)

2016 – CURRENT

Raffie is our current black Labrador, and came to join our family in March 2017, shortly after the passing of our angel Holly. We could see that Ruby was sad after losing her mate of over 10 years. We knew we wanted another Labrador, but we were not sure, due to Ruby being nearly 11 years old, whether our next baby should be a puppy or one a little older. After some investigation, we came across Raffie. He was about 9 months old and was looking for a new home, he was supposed to become a support dog for children with autism, but as the current owners said, he was not concentrating on his training and they decided that he was not suitable to meet their strict requirements. He originally resided on the Sunshine Coast and had to be flown down to us in Victoria. On meeting him, we instantly fell in love with him. We expected him to be a little out of sorts and nervous after his big flight ordeal, but we were so surprised to see him so happy and loving. He settled into our home very quickly.

Ruby loved him and appreciated the company, although at 9 months he was still a handful and she did her very best to keep him under control for us. Our cats on the other hand took a little longer to accept this new member. Macey, by this stage was nearly 14.5 years old and getting quite chilled out, accepted him fairly quickly.

Fletcher on the other hand, did not and never did learn to like Raffie at all. Fletcher would not interact with Raffie at all. Whenever Raffie is inside, Fletcher would go away and hide.

Raffie, although now nearly 6 years old, has by far been our biggest challenge. He has been quite a handful and has rightfully earned his nickname "Mr Vandal Pants"

BBQ CAPERS

Although we are not much for having BBQ's at home, we do own a BBQ and had a cover to protect it from the elements. It is a BBQ which sits on its own little cabinet which has magnetic doors.

This cover was something that both Holly and Ruby never touched. However, it was no match for Master Raffie.

One day, I came home to find a big mess under the outdoor alfresco area. Raffie had successfully been able to chew and pull the BBQ cover apart and it was now in pieces all over our outdoor deck.

That was not the only interesting thing that I found. Somehow, he had managed to open the magnetic doors of the storage cabinet under the BBQ and completely empty it of a roll of paper towel and BBQ cleaning brush. We still cannot work out how he was smart enough to open these doors.

As the BBQ was now unprotected, his attention then turned to the Burner knobs, and he successfully pulled these off the BBQ and began to chew them up also. Granted this was not all in the one day, but over several days. We managed to rescue some of the burner knobs before they were all destroyed.

So we now have what you would call a "Claytons BBQ" the BBQ you have when you don't have a

BBQ. It is sitting there without knobs or a protective cover.

"NO MORE LAUNDRY MUM!"

Raffie's fascination with knobs did not stop with the BBQ, our laundry by night becomes the doggie's bedroom.   We have a front loader washing machine which has a protruding control knob in the top face of the machine.

You can imagine what this story is about.

Morning time comes and I open the laundry door and greet both Ruby and Raffie and let them out for their morning wees, and get them ready for breakfast.

As I walk to the back door, I noticed some chewed up material on the floor. I look down, pick it up and try to work out what it was. Then my eyes spotted this gaping hole in the front of my washing machine.

I couldn't believe my eyes, Oh no, I thought, the machine was broken for good, how were we going to fix this.

My husband was also not amused, he had just arrived home from night shift so was not able to do anything at that point in time.

I went out later that morning and my husband sent me a message that the knob obviously did not agree with Raffie and he had actually vomited some of it up in the laundry that I had not seen at the time of letting him out in the morning.

I was in shock by this vandalism of Raffie's and being a member of Facebook, I decided to put a photo of Raffie's latest disaster on Facebook, I tried to take a photo with my phone but for some reason, it was not loading on Facebook, I kept walking in and out of the laundry, to get a photo that worked, little did I know that each time I walked in and out to get photos, I was only centimetres away from stepping in the vomit that Raffie had left.

Luckily the spindle of the control was still intact and could be turned, so the machine was still able to be used.

We ordered a new knob and once that arrived a protective wooden cover was built to sit over the top of the machine to protect the knob from any future attacks.

RAFFIE SORTS THE TOWELS IN THE LINEN CUPBOARD

Raffie had woken up before the rest of the house on a weekend, and was still in the laundry. Ruby being the older of the 2 was still sleeping in the laundry with him.   Raffie became bored and looked for something to do.   Our linen cupboard is in the laundry and he decided to investigate what was in this cupboard.

He used his paws and mouth to open up the doors and managed to get in to the cupboard and proceeded to look in and see what mischief he could find to entertain himself until the rest of the house woke up.

He was able to reach the shelf that contained all the towels and one by one began pulling them out onto the floor. We have a security camera in the laundry and we later watched him doing this.

We could see him disappear behind the open door, and then saw towels piling up on the floor. He would occasionally stop and look around to the door that led to the house to check if the coast was still clear. Once he was satisfied it was, he continued emptying the shelves. He didn't chew any towels, he just pulled them out into a pile on the floor. All the while, Ruby remained asleep and in no way was a party to his unruly behaviour.

We couldn't believe our eyes when we opened the door a little while later and saw the cupboard doors open and our towels all over the floor.

We then had to devise a way to secure these doors so they could not be opened again. We ended up buying child door locks and placing them over the handles so they could not be unintentionally opened by furry thieves.

KARAH

2019 – CURRENT

Our most recent canine addition to our family is our yellow Labrador Karah, who arrived about 5 years ago at the age of 10 weeks old. She came to us from a family who due to work commitments were unable to give this young girl the attention that she needed. She helped all of us, especially Raffie ease the pain of losing Ruby who had recently passed away.

Raffie and Karah became fast friends and together are a dynamic duo of fun and entertainment for us.

Our cats accept Karah, even Fletcher is not as scared of Karah as he is of Raffie, maybe because she is the same color as our previous yellow girl Holly, who he grew up with.

Karah is an extremely affectionate loving ball of energy.

KARAH THE DANCER

Karah shows us so much love and is always so excited to see us when we arrive home from work or an outing. She will meet us at the gate and jump on her hind legs and jump up and down as if dancing with excitement that we are home.

If Raffie is not immediately there when we arrive home she will race off around the back of house to find him and escort him back to the gate where she will continue her dance routine.

Seeing this, it is impossible not to laugh and smile at her and acknowledge her dance steps, so it has been reinforced I guess and now is a daily occurrence.

KARAH THE CUDDLER

Karah, although a very active young girl and just 3 years old, absolutely loves her cuddles

Of an evening, she has no hesitation to jump up on my lap in the chair and settle down for cuddles. She truly believes she is a lap dog. She has been known to cuddle for hours stretched out, even upside down on my lap.

We can just see the love she has for us in her eyes, and the way she runs towards us whenever she sees us.

Her extreme love can sometimes catch us off guard and she has been known to launch herself at us and can be a bit rough at times.

Also we find that whenever we kneel down on the ground, either to do some weeding in the garden, or anything at floor level, this is like an open invitation to Karah.

She will come rushing over and rub all over us, nuzzling us for cuddles. It is like the fact that we are down at her level we are open game for cuddles and play.

There is no use in trying to ignore this, any attempts to do so are futile and only met with more persistent nuzzling.

Needless to say, that anything we attempt to do at ground level with Karah around takes longer than anticipated and is always full of lots of cuddles and kisses.

MAGGIE

2023 – CURRENT

Due to the extremely strong bond that my husband shared with our last cat Fletcher, he was reluctant to welcome another cat into our lives but after a lot of gentle persistent persuasion on my part, he finally agreed and earlier this year, we decided to add another feline to our household. My husband and I both had some health issues requiring surgery unfortunately both at the same time earlier this year, and we felt that a new cat would be a reward for the difficult times we had both gone through. I contacted a local cat rescue and the very next day we went to view this little girl who at that time was only about 5 months old. My husband being the loving cat person he is, instantly fell in love with this little girl, who was originally named Oren by her foster carer. The decision was made, she was coming home with us, and we changed her name to Maggie.

Understandably, she was initially very nervous and took a couple of days to trust us and to love us and her new home. Every day, she brightens our lives with her super affectionate nature, extra loud purr and mischievous nature.

NO TRESPASSERS ALLOWED

Maggie quickly settled into our home and is very confident and loving with us and our two dogs, Raffie and Karah. In no time at all she has become the boss of the household and is not shy in telling us and the dogs what she wants.

We have a separate lounge room in the house set up with her cat toys and due to different tv viewing, my husband will spend most nights in the separate lounge area watching his shows. Maggie happily joins him in there. On many occasions, Maggie has become territorial of this room and will eagerly chase me or the dogs out of this room if she feels we are trespassing in her and her Dad's space. She will chase us out and then proceed to jump on the door from the inside in an attempt to close the door shutting us out, It is like she is saying to us "Get out, and stay out!"

Life is Better with
a Yellow Lab

CONCLUSION

Over the years, I have been so lucky to have so many beautiful animals come into my life and share many experiences with me. They may only share our lives for a short time, but however long it is, is truly magical. Each one has been different, having their own special personality and traits. The common thread with all of them, are they have all been truly loving and all hold a special place in my heart and the hearts of my family for ever.

They have all taught us many different things including patience, responsibility and have always provided us with true love and enjoyment.

My animals have always been happy, loving, and always my best friends in life.

If everyone had a personality similar to that of our animals the world would truly be a beautiful place.